Pizarro

by Benjamin Felker

No one shall commit or authorize any act or omission by which the copyright of, or the right to copyright, this play may be impaired.

No one shall make any changes in this play for the purpose of production.

Publication of this play does not imply availability for performance. Both amateurs and professionals considering a production are strongly advised in their own interests to apply to Samuel French, Inc., for written permission before starting rehearsals, advertising, or booking a theatre.

No part of this book may be reproduced, stored in a retrieval system, or transmitted in any form, by any means, now known or yet to be invented, including mechanical, electronic, photocopying, recording, videotaping, or otherwise, without the prior written permission of the publisher.

MUSIC USE NOTE

Licensees are solely responsible for obtaining formal written permission from copyright owners to use copyrighted music in the performance of this play and are strongly cautioned to do so. If no such permission is obtained by the licensee, then the licensee must use only original music that the licensee owns and controls. Licensees are solely responsible and liable for all music clearances and shall indemnify the copyright owners of the play and their licensing agent, Samuel French, Inc., against any costs, expenses, losses and liabilities arising from the use of music by licensees.

IMPORTANT BILLING AND CREDIT REQUIREMENTS

All producers of *PIZARRO must* give credit to the Author of the Play in all programs distributed in connection with performances of the Play, and in all instances in which the title of the Play appears for the purposes of advertising, publicizing or otherwise exploiting the Play and/or a production. The name of the Author *must* appear on a separate line on which no other name appears, immediately following the title and *must* appear in size of type not less than fifty percent of the size of the title type.

CHARACTERS

MARIA PIZARRO - Francisco Pizarro's niece.

FRANCISCO PIZARRO - Just returned from an expedition with Balboa and now wants to search for gold in Peru.

DIEGO DE ALMAGRO - Pizarro's partner on an expedition to Peru.

HERNANDO DE SOTO - a young explorer on Pizarro's team.

BARTOLOMEO RUIZ - a navigator who accompanies Pizarro to Peru.

VASCO NUNEZ DE BALBOA - a Spanish explorer, arrested for treason.

GUARD

MANCO - an Incan who later helps lead a revolt against Pizarro.

TUPAC - an Incan.

CHANCA - An Incan, Tupac's wife.

ATAHUALPA - new chief of the Incas, after civil war, referred to as the Sapa Inca.

VOICE - announces the approach of the great Sapa Inca.

ATAHUALPA'S ATTENDANTS

FRANCISCO ALMAGRO - Diego Almagro's son

AN INCAN BARTENDER

PIZARRO was the winner of the 2005 Baker's Plays High School Playwrighting Competition.

Scene 1:
Spanish Town

*(**MARIA** and **RUIZ** are chatting in the street as they wait for **BALBOA**.)*

MARIA. Señor Ruiz, what is happening? There is a great crowd, and many guards!

RUIZ. Ah, Maria – ever the curious one. The famous Balboa is coming. The crowd has heard of his explorations of the New World, but the governor does not like him. Balboa has tried repeatedly to oust the Governor of Castile, but unsuccessfully.

*(**BALBOA** enters, flanked by **PIZARRO**. A **GUARD** walks up to **BALBOA**.)*

GUARD. Captain Balboa?

BALBOA. *(vainly)* Balboa, that's me!! Vasco N.!!

GUARD. You're under arrest. Charges: a threat to the governor.

BALBOA. Did you say, Balboa? That's him!

*(points at **PIZARRO** who darts to his left)*

Ah, that's him!

*(looks to his left, **PIZARRO** darts to his right)*

All right, it's me. But I'm innocent!!

GUARD. Yeah, yeah, they all say that!!

*(**GUARD** drags **BALBOA** away.)*

MARIA. Can they really do that? Take a man away just because the governor doesn't like him?

RUIZ. When something is in the way of what a man wants, he'll find a way to get it.

(**MARIA** *and* **RUIZ** *exit, and* **PIZARRO** *remains and* **ALMAGRO** *enters.*)

PIZARRO. My old amigo! Diego de Almagro! How are you? Enjoying retirement?

ALMAGRO. Francisco Pizarro! It's been too long! Retirement? I hate it. I'm itching for a nice violent expedition. I hate processing tax returns. Speaking of expeditions, how'd yours go? Find any gold when you were out there with Balboa?

PIZARRO. That's just what I wanted to talk to you about. See this?

(hands an object to **ALMAGRO***)*

This gold idol I got from an Indian over in Panama. He said it came from far south in the Americas, from a golden city, where precious objects of this kind are as common as stones in the street. Oh, Diego, an expedition over there could turn out to be the richest ever!!

ALMAGRO. How do you know this Indian was telling the truth?

PIZARRO. I have never known an Indian to lie. I've been in Mexico with Cortez and in Panama with Balboa, and I have never known an Indian who lied.

ALMAGRO. All right. Let's do it. Did this Indian tell you how far this place was? Does it have an army? What sort of weapons?

PIZARRO. I have told you all I know. I talked to him just before Balboa threw him to the dogs.

ALMAGRO. Well, we'll have to do a bit of exploring. Wait. We're going to split this fifty fifty aren't we partner?

PIZARRO. Right. Equal partnership.

(He exits.)

*(***ALMAGRO*** ponders the impending expedition.)*

ALMAGRO. Ah, such a pretty thing. Balboa has come the closest of all of us to striking it rich. Ahh, gold. A small, short word that holds all men in its thrall. A simple peseta can buy a beer or a loaf of bread, or it can buy any man's friendship. A man can do anything if he has enough gold. I wonder…how much gold will this new expedition generate. What will be my reward? A million? Ten million? What if I were promoted to be governor, or captain, or head honcho? Then I'd have as much gold as I want!! What should be my title? "Head Honcho of the Southern Lands?" Nah, something more noble sounding…"Lord of the Golden South." Yes I like that! Ah – looks like Francisco has already rounded up some stout men.

(**PIZARRO** *enters, leading* **RUIZ**, **MARIA**, *and* **DE SOTO**.)

PIZARRO. Mi Amigo! I have a crew. First let me introduce Bartolomeo Ruiz, an expert navigator. Then there is Hernando de Soto. He holds the title of National Dueling Champion. A fine man with a good sword. And last but not least, my niece, Maria Pizarro.

ALMAGRO. *(disapprovingly)* A girl? And so young. What is your age, señorita?

MARIA. Fifteen, sir.

PIZARRO. My brother, her father, died three years ago in the Castile riot. He appointed me legal guardian. She'll do the cooking!

ALMAGRO. All right, then. It's settled. I will purchase a ship and we'll all get going.

(They all begin exiting.)

What do you say next Wednesday?

Scene 2:
A Shoreline in Panama

(The camp is set up. **RUIZ** *and* **ALMAGRO** *are playing cards.* **MARIA** *is tending the fire and* **PIZARRO** *is sitting on a rock, obviously waiting for something.)*

RUIZ. I dealt. So it's your turn.

ALMAGRO. All right. Give me all your fours.

RUIZ. Sorry. Out of luck. Go hunt!

MARIA. Hey you guys. It's "Go fish!", not "Go hunt!"

RUIZ. Whatever. Okay, Almagro. Gimme your jacks.

MARIA. How *do* you get Chicken Noodle soup out of the can?

PIZARRO. Use the chisel in the tool pouch. Over there, by the glass beads.

ALMAGRO. I wonder why it's taking so long to get permission from the governor of Panama so we can proceed with the expedition?

*(***DE SOTO** *enters with a message.)*

DE SOTO. Here is the message, sir.

*(***PIZARRO** *looks at it and hand it back.)*

PIZARRO. Here, you read it to me.

DE SOTO. *(reads)* From the new governor, the Honorable Don Pedro de los Rios. To the idiotic fools who insist on tramping around trying to topple ancient kingdoms for their gold, in other words, Pizarro and his crew.

PIZARRO. New governor? A lot has changed since I was back here in Panama.

DE SOTO. *(reads)* I do not approve of this expedition, therefore, I have seen fit to withdraw my political support. But don't let that stop you! Keep going, and get yourselves killed! It'll rid us of your troublesome hides. Sincerely, or not, I remain Governor of Panama, Don Pedro de los Rios.

PIZARRO. *(resolved)* So, what do we do now, men? I'll tell you! *(draws sword, makes line in road)* Comrades, on that side, to the south are toil, hunger, the drenching storm, desertion, and death. On this side, ease and pleasure. There lies Peru and its riches, here lies Panama and its poverty. Choose, comrades, what most befits a brave Castilian. For my part – I go to the South! *(jumps over the line)* Who's with me?

RUIZ. I am, sir! Look out, Indians, Bartolomeo Ruiz is coming! *(jumps over the line)*

ALMAGRO. I'm with you, partner!

DE SOTO and **MARIA**. *(unison)* We're coming too! *(jump over line)*

PIZARRO. Great! Pack up, everyone! Here's our plan: we travel South, make our presence as little known as possible. Then we test the strength of the natives. Let's get going! Ruiz – direction!

RUIZ. *(looking at compass)* Thataway, sir.

DE SOTO. That's the bay. We either swim it or walk around it!

MARIA. Or get on the ship and sail to the other side!

ALMAGRO. What do you think, Francisco?

PIZARRO. Let's walk around it. I'm going to need the exercise.

(All exit, with noses in the air.)

Scene 3:
An Indian Village

(**TUPAC** *and* **CHANCA** *are onstage.*)

TUPAC. Times have changed, have they not, Chanca?

CHANCA. Indeed, Tupac, they have changed much. If only Huayna Capac was still alive.

TUPAC. Yes! Ever since he died, those two sons of his, Huascar and Atahualpa, have been going at it hammer and tongs. Atahualpa doesn't care that Huascar was named heir to the throne.

CHANCA. No, he takes his large army from Ecuador and tries to take the throne by force.

TUPAC. No good will come of this civil war. Our armies are weak. What will happen if our neighbors, the Araucanian Indians, see our weakness and strike?

CHANCA. We shall surely fall. Even Huayna Capac who conquered Ecuador and Colombia could not overcome the Araucanians. Oh my…look…it's Manco!

(**MANCO** *runs in, breathing heavily.*)

TUPAC. What is it, Manco?

MANCO. Strangers, sir. Pale strangers with great beards of hair growing from their chins! They wear shiny clothes that spears cannot pierce. Their weapons are hard and sharp. We are doomed.

TUPAC. Go, Manco, and warn the Sapa Inca.

(**MANCO** *exits hastily.*)

Chanca, you must take the baby and flee to Cuzco. Stay with your uncle. I shall follow later.

CHANCA. But, Tupac…

TUPAC. Just go!

(**TUPAC** *hands bag to* **CHANCA** *and* **CHANCA** *exits.* **TUPAC** *shoves things into a sack and takes his weapon.* **ALMAGRO** *and* **DE SOTO** *enter.*)

DE SOTO. *(doesn't see* **TUPAC** *at first)* Where could the rest of the crew be?

ALMAGRO. I don't know! It was Pizarro's idea to go in pincer formation. He got lost. Or we got lost.

TUPAC. The pale strangers!

ALMAGRO. Hey, you! Come on, Hernando, let's take him!

> *(***ALMAGRO*** *rushes* ***TUPAC.*** *A short swift sword fight ensues.* ***TUPAC*** *gets* ***ALMAGRO*** *in the eye.)*

ALMAGRO. Ow! My eye!

> *(***DE SOTO*** *steps up and disarms* ***TUPAC.****)*

DE SOTO. What's your name, Injun?

TUPAC. I am called Tupac, honorable one…

> *(***MARIA*** *and* ***RUIZ*** *enter.)*

More pale ones!

> *(***MARIA*** *tends to* ***ALMAGRO.****)*

RUIZ. Good work, De Soto. I see you have a prisoner. What is your capital city?

TUPAC. Cuzco, my Lord.

RUIZ. Who is your king?

TUPAC. Atahualpa, at the moment, your lordship.

ALMAGRO. What do you mean "at the moment?" Ow, Maria. Go easy!

TUPAC. It is a civil war. Two brothers fight for sovereignty. Atahualpa is on top right now.

DE SOTO. This information will be most interesting to Pizarro. Tupac, may our leaders meet?

TUPAC. I shall tell my ruler you desire it so. My nephew Manco shall bring you his answer.

ALMAGRO. Then go. Post haste! *(groans)*

> *(***TUPAC*** *rushes offstage.)*

RUIZ. This will be great! "Cuzco." Doesn't that just sound rich to you, Almagro? *(pokes around, finds and picks up a bag of gold)* Just as we thought! This place is loaded with gold!

ALMAGRO. Yes. Ow! Oh, be careful! One would think you knew nothing of eye wounds?

MARIA. I don't.

(She places a patch on ALMAGRO's eye.)

There. He's just blind in one eye. That's all.

DE SOTO. You look like a real pirate!

ALMAGRO. Yes, but I'll never again be able to draw a bow.

RUIZ. Could you ever draw a bow?

ALMAGRO. That's *(groan)* beside the point.

MARIA. Sorry!

DE SOTO. Has anyone seen Pizarro? Where could he be?

(PIZARRO enters.)

PIZARRO. Oh, there you are. I've just been run over by a mad Indian. He was blabbering on about "pale strangers desiring to meet with the Inca." You know what he's talking about?

ALMAGRO. We're the strangers, Francisco. That Indian gave us valuable information on the state of things around here.

DE SOTO. There is a civil war going on. But look at this gold!

PIZARRO. How opportunistic! Finally!

ALMAGRO. *(with an angry glance at DE SOTO)* Yes, *(groan)*, we have arranged for a meeting with their ruler.

PIZARRO. Diego, mi amigo, what happened to your eye?

ALMAGRO. I got worsted in a fight. Anyway, we meet with their ruler and then what? What's the next step, oh partner-with-the-plan?

PIZARRO. Well, let's see. Ruiz, go get a messenger from our reserve point and tell him to take this pot of gold to King Charles and ask for royal commissions. Meanwhile we go and see if they'll surrender without a fight. Then we'll go from there.

(RUIZ exits.)

MARIA. Oh, look. Here comes a messenger.

MANCO. Glorious strangers. I bring the Inca's reply. He awaits your visit with great interest. Proceed directly to Cajamarca.

PIZARRO. Tell him we're on our way.

*(The group follows **MANCO.**)*

Scene 4:
Market Square

(**PIZARRO**, **ALMAGRO**, **DE SOTO** *on a horse,* **MARIA***, and* **MANCO** *enter, admiring the beauty of Cajamarca.*)

SPANIARDS. *(in unison)* Wow!

MANCO. Magnificent, is it not?

ALMAGRO. Indeed. The architecture is unique.

PIZARRO. *(eagerly)* Yes, yes. Very nice, I'm sure. Where is the Inca, as you call him.

MANCO. Patience, your whiteness. Remember, the Inca is the ruler and he is coming of his own will. Ah – here he is now.

VOICE. Attention, other-worldly strangers. The moment is nigh when you should meet Atahualpa, The Father of the People, the Face of Greatness. The Sapa Inca of the Land of the four Quarters, also known as the Land of the dollar.

ALMAGRO. Dollar?

VOICE. Yes. Don't four quarters make a dollar? Anyway. Behold the Inca!

(**ATAHUALPA** *enters, flanked by attendants.*)

PIZARRO. Greetings, Atahualpa, old chap. You've done a great job, governing the place for us until we can take over.

ATAHUALPA. What? Who said I was giving up the throne?

PIZARRO. The great King Charles the fifth.

ATAHUALPA. How is it he's so great if I have never heard of him?

PIZARRO. He has just now decided to reveal himself to you.

ATAHUALPA. *(looking at* **DE SOTO***'s horse),* Is that an animal? It is wondrous powerful.

DE SOTO. *(astride the horse)* Then watch what it can do.

(**DE SOTO** *rides around daringly and charges* **ATAHUALPA** *and attendants. Attendants run away screaming but* **ATAHUALPA** *stands firm.*)

ATAHUALPA. Very nice. Is there anything you need at the present that I can provide? You may stay in the city.

(**ATAHUALPA** *exits, beckoning to* **MANCO** *to follow.*)

DE SOTO. Wow, he didn't even blink when I almost ran him over.

MARIA. A good, brave, king.

ALMAGRO. What happened? A fly flew into my good eye and I missed the whole thing.

DE SOTO. Pizarro, sir, maybe I could talk alone with the Inca. I might be able to negotiate an agreement in our favor. No harm trying.

PIZARRO. All right.

(**DE SOTO** *exits.*)

Now crew, what we need to do here is capture Atahualpa. Remember how Cortez won Mexico by capturing the Aztec emperor? That's what we'll do. Now, how do we set this up? Cortez invited the emperor to a banquet.

ALMAGRO. A knife at his throat would create a hostage situation and we could ask for a ransom. I'll bet these Peruvians would do anything for their king!

PIZARRO. Right! Get some sleep, everyone. We'll send a message on the morrow.

Scene 5:
Market at Night

(ATAHUALPA *strolls in pondering his country's plight.*
DE SOTO *enters and joins him.*)

DE SOTO. Good evening, sir Inca.

ATAHUALPA. Ah, yes, good evening, Mr. Horse Rider.

DE SOTO. You like that, huh? Call me Hernando, or De
Soto, or Peanut.

ATAHUALPA. Peanut?

DESOTO. My mommy used to call me that…

ATAHUALPA. Why have you come to take my empire, which
I have worked so hard to obtain? What do you want so
much that you lay waste to my countryside?

DE SOTO. First of all, our king told us to conquer you.
Second, you have much of that we value highly.

ATAHUALPA. What is that?

DE SOTO. Gold. As one of our generals said, "We Spaniards
suffer from a disease of the heart which alone can be
cured by gold." With enough gold a Spaniard can get
anything he wants. That's not always a good thing.

ATAHUALPA. That's funny. Here, there is a lot of gold. But
you Spaniards have a lot of things we Incas don't – like
steel armor, and horses.

DE SOTO. I noticed you didn't flinch when I approached,
unlike your attendants.

ATAHUALPA. And I had them executed immediately for
showing fear before the strangers.

DE SOTO. You certainly have high standards.

ATAHUALPA. High? Of course they're high! I'm descended
from the sun god! I'm where everyone turns for help!
The buck stops here!

DE SOTO. Yes, well, I came here to propose a deal. Our
king sent us here to add your Land of the Four
Quarters to his Spanish Empire. If you acknowledge

his sovereignty over you and your lands, there will be a lot less bloodshed and you might retain much of your current command.

ATAHUALPA. But that would mean giving up all I fought for all these years.

DE SOTO. Sir Inca, I admire you and your gallant dedication. But you can see you are no match to our armor, horses, and swords.

ATAHUALPA. Not all the country would comply so peacefully. There will be rebellions no matter what. However, I feel that I should consider your proposal. I am weary. Good night.

DE SOTO. Good night, your highness. Stay in touch.

(**ATAHUALPA** *exits.*)

What a guy!

(**DE SOTO** *exits.*)

Scene 6:
Market in the Morning

(**PIZARRO**, **ALMAGRO**, *and* **MARIA** *enter.* **PIZARRO** *holds map, spreads it out and examines it with the others.*)

PIZARRO. All right. See, this is where we are now. Over here is where the Sapa Inca will enter the courtyard and we'll meet him right over here. Maria, you'll be preparing the food, okay?

MARIA. Aye Aye, Uncle!

PIZARRO. Hernando – you'll…where is Hernando De Soto?

ALMAGRO. He was out late last night talking with Atahualpa. Here he comes…

(**DE SOTO** *enters.*)

DE SOTO. Wow! I slept in. All right, Captain, what's the buzz?

PIZARRO. You were out late last night talking with Atahualpa. Did you persuade him to surrender peacefully?

DE SOTO. He said the people might not like it, but he would consider the proposal.

PIZARRO. We shall capture him if he does not surrender. I'll invite him to a banquet, and then we'll see who has mastery over the situation.

DE SOTO. You won't kill him, will you?

ALMAGRO. Of course not. Think of the ransoms we could get!

PIZARRO. De Soto you'll be stationed over here in ambush and when…

RUIZ. What's my assignment?

PIZARRO. You'll go over here. When the Inca arrives, we'll ask him to surrender. When he refuses, you and De Soto will rush over and capture him. Maria – get cooking. De Soto – you invite him over for dinner.

DE SOTO. Right.

(**DE SOTO** *exits.*)

ALMAGRO. What do I do? A little dance?

PIZARRO. Sure! What a great idea! Can you do the chicken dance? That's my favorite!

ALMAGRO. *(annoyed)* I was kidding. What do you want me to do?

PIZARRO. As my right hand man, you will be here with me. We will welcome the Inca together.

MARIA. *(calling from the cooking area)* What shall we serve? Pasta alfredo? Pork Flambé? How about leftover Chef Boyardee Ravioli?

PIZARRO and **RUIZ**. *(in unison)* Tacos!!

MARIA. Okay. We'll need that cow you plundered, Ruiz. I'll need some lettuce, cheese and tortillas. No tomatoes though. They're poisonous!

RUIZ. They sure are! I saw a man eat a tomato once. He got up when it was done and slam! He got run over by a horse! Died the next day, poor soul.

(*The team all cross themselves.*)

ALMAGRO. Can we make a little hot sauce? I like my tacos spicy!

MARIA. Sure!

(**DE SOTO** *enters.*)

DE SOTO. It's done. The Inca has been invited and has accepted the invitation. Is that tacos I smell?

PIZARRO. It is almost time. Places everyone. Hernando, come here. I know you are a friend of the Inca. Take this knife. When you capture the Inca, use it to persuade him that we mean business. Don't need to draw blood, just hold it at his throat.

DE SOTO. But sir…as you wish.

PIZARRO. Go to your position.

(**RUIZ** *and* **DE SOTO** *are in ambush.* **MARIA** *is setting the table, and* **PIZARRO** *and* **ALMAGRO** *are sitting in chairs.*)

VOICE. Introducing the great Sapa Inca, Lord of all Peru!

PIZARRO. At last.

(**ATAHUALPA** *enters.*)

Lord Inca, we welcome your presence at our humble feast. But first, business. You have thought much on our proposal of peaceful surrender?

ATAHUALPA. Much. For me, it is a lose-lose situation. If I surrender, I either retire to the country or be provincial governor. The people would feel that I had deserted them. They would murder me. On the other hand, if I refuse to surrender, I will be hailed as a hero of patriotism but warfare would ravage my already war-torn lands. Surrender means revolts, refusal means war. I will be a patriot. I succumb to nationalism. I refuse to let strangers order me around! I reject your offer, come what may!

PIZARRO. It will come! You are my prisoner!

(**RUIZ** *and* **DE SOTO** *hold knives to* **ATAHUALPA.**)

You have rejected our peaceful offer. You leave us with no choice but to carry out our king's command. We will conquer! You, meanwhile will be our prisoner until we have a satisfactory ransom!

ALMAGRO. You can eat your tacos in the cell! Take him away!

(**RUIZ** *and* **DE SOTO** *take* **ATAHUALPA** *offstage. Lights darken.*)

Scene 7:
Hut

(DE SOTO and ATAHUALPA are playing chess. ATAHUALPA is chained around the neck.)

DE SOTO. Ooh, good move. Let's see. I'll do that.

ATAHUALPA. Very interesting. You Spaniards have great imaginations, inventing all sorts of things from practical tools to wonderful games like this one. What's it called again? Chings?

DE SOTO. No, it's called chess. We didn't invent it. Good move. Hmmm. Ah! Your bishop's open! I'll take him.

ATAHUALPA. You left your knight unprotected so I'll capture him.

DE SOTO. I saw that coming. I was hoping you wouldn't notice it. You think that we'll want a real big ransom? I'll move this pawn.

ATAHUALPA. I wouldn't be surprised. If your leaders want gold as much as you say they do, they won't hesitate. I'll bring out my rook.

DE SOTO. Good move. Look out, here comes my knight! What'll you do when you get free?

ATAHUALPA. Well, I think…

(PIZARRO and ALMAGRO enter.)

ALMAGRO. All right, enough fun time. Pack it up De Soto. We and the Inca have business to do.

(DE SOTO picks up the pieces and leaves.)

PIZARRO. Okay, Atahualpa. You know what we want. Gold. Lots of it. What do you think your people will pay to have you free?

ATAHUALPA. Take this collar off and I'll show you!

(ATAHUALPA leads them to the doors and opens one of them.)

My people will fill this room up to as high as I can reach with gold. *(crosses to next door)* This room will be filled the same way, twice over with silver. Is that a satisfactory ransom?

ALMAGRO. *(aside to* **PIZARRO***)* That's a lot. I don't think they can get that much!

PIZARRO. *(aside to* **ALMAGRO***)* If they can't it's to our advantage. *(to* **ATAHUALPA***)* We'll take your offer.

ATAHUALPA. You'll let me go?

PIZARRO. If we get the ransom.

ATAHUALPA. You will. I'll write to my people. They will send the valuables.

PIZARRO. Go. Write. Don't try any funny business. I'll have someone read your letters.

*(***PIZARRO*** snaps his fingers and* **RUIZ** *enters and takes* **ATAHUALPA** *offstage.)*

ALMAGRO. That ransom is impossibly big! He must be desperate. He's trying to pull something, Francisco. I know it.

PIZARRO. If it comes, we can't let him go. We'll have to kill him. He wants to be free but revolts will follow.

ALMAGRO. De Soto will be a problem. He's getting too friendly with the Inca. We'll have to get rid of him too.

PIZARRO. And then the Inca will be out of our way.

(Both laugh evil laughs and then exit.)

Scene 8:
Pizarro's Table at the Palace

RUIZ. My captain, I have here the report from King Charles.

(**RUIZ** *hands* **PIZARRO** *the report and then exits.*)

PIZARRO. Good. Here you read it. I never learned how.

ALMAGRO. I'm sorry, but I can't read it either!

PIZARRO. You can't read or write? I'll call Maria. She can read. Maria!

(**MARIA** *enters.*)

MARIA. Yes, Uncle.

PIZARRO. Read this, por favor.

MARIA. *(reading)* "To the illustrious and dashing hero, Francisco Pizarro, and his dutiful side kick, Diego de Almagro. Greetings. This message is meant to mete out the rewards earned by my faithful conquistadors. To Pizarro, go all the lands to govern in my name, and all the gold he can claim. Pizarro shall receive the title 'Royal Governor' and 'Head Honcho of Peru'. To Almagro, he shall receive gold and shall be the mayor of Tombes and be Pizarro's sidekick and second-in-command."

ALMAGRO. Ha ha, very funny. You're joking, right?

MARIA. No.

ALMAGRO. You have to be.

MARIA. Sorry. That's what it says. See? Read it for yourself!

ALMAGRO. I can't read! *(to* **PIZARRO***)* You and I were equal partners. I should get an equal share! I demand my rightful inheritance! Give me my rightful share! I've been shorted and gypped! I lost my eye fighting fairly while you were cowering around in the woods! It's not fair!

(**ALMAGRO** *storms off.*)

PIZARRO. He's a little upset.

MARIA. Do you blame him?

*(**RUIZ** enters.)*

RUIZ. Sir, there is so much gold. Indians have been coming in all day! Silver too! More of them than I have ever seen in my whole life! There's enough to fill three rooms with precious things! It's worth billions!

MARIA. The ransom.

PIZARRO. Bring De Soto to me. *(**RUIZ** exits.)* I've a special task for him.

MARIA. What is it?

PIZARRO. You've noticed the growing friendship between him and the Inca?

MARIA. Yes.

PIZARRO. I'm going to get him out of my way. Watch!

*(**RUIZ** and **DE SOTO** enter.)*

DE SOTO. What is it you desire of me, my Captain?

PIZARRO. You have been selected, De Soto. Almagro and I have decided that you are the best person to assign to this important task.

DE SOTO. *(cautiously)* Which is…

PIZARRO. You shall guard and accompany the King's share of the treasure. You must make sure it reaches Spain safely. The King will reward you. Remember the treasure must be safe!

DE SOTO. I will perform this task with all my skill, sir. The treasure will reach the King safely, with my sword keeping it safe. When shall I embark?

PIZARRO. At once. Your horse awaits you. You have been packed up and your men are waiting.

*(**DE SOTO** bows and leaves.)*

Ruiz, make sure he is on his way, and bring me the Inca.

*(**RUIZ** exits and returns with **ATAHUALPA**.)*

ATAHUALPA. I and my people have kept our end of the bargain. You have three rooms full of precious metals. Now, free me, as you promised.

PIZARRO. No.

ATAHUALPA, RUIZ, and **MARIA**. *(in unison)* What!

ATAHUALPA. You Spaniards have no honor. At least I keep my word. Even to my enemies.

RUIZ. Sir, I do not agree to this madness!

MARIA. Uncle – you gave him your word!

PIZARRO. Enough! Am I not in charge here? Ruiz, take him to the executioner!

RUIZ. I must obey you but what you do is wrong.

PIZARRO. Ruiz! Take him away NOW or it won't be just the Inca's head rolling on the ground!

(**RUIZ** *and* **ATAHUALPA** *exit.*)

MARIA. Uncle! How can you do this? Atahualpa kept his word and you kill him? How can you justify it?

PIZARRO. Maria, imagine for a moment that you rule a great empire and your people love you. Then an army captures you and holds you for ransom. What will be the first thing you do when they see you free?

MARIA. Why organize a revolt, of course and try to use my own people to regain independence.

PIZARRO. Exactly.

MARIA. And that was why you had to get rid of De Soto. He wouldn't have let you kill his friend.

PIZARRO. Precisely. Now all this gold is MINE. I am the sole ruler! All power is MINE!

MARIA. Uncle, you have turned into a greedy fool. You killed all those Peruvians for your own benefit?

PIZARRO. I prefer to see it as bringing civilization to those savages.

(**MARIA** *walks off, bumping into* **MANCO** *who is carrying a tray of drinks.*)

MANCO. Excuse me. Your drinks, master.

PIZARRO. Thank you, Manco. Manco, have you ever envied the Inca?

MANCO. No, sir.

PIZARRO. Oh. Well, Atahualpa died recently and I am appointing you as Sapa Inca. And you will take your orders from me.

MANCO. Yes, master. Whatever you say.

PIZARRO. Good. Clear the dishes and dust my table. I am going out to supervise the building of my new city.

(**PIZARRO** *exits and* **MANCO** *does as asked.*)

MANCO. *(to himself)* Atahualpa dead! And I am appointed to succeed him! I see their minds. I am but a puppet ruler. "You shall take your orders from me." What kind of llama does he think I am? I will retreat into the mountains and form an underground resistance. I'll launch attacks…wait patience. Don't be hasty. Make sure Atahualpa's death is not for nothing.

(**MANCO** *exits.*)

Scene 9:
Bar, Many Months Later

(**ALMAGRO** *and* **DE SOTO** *are sitting at the bar. An Indian bartender pours drinks.*)

DE SOTO. Two root beers.

ALMAGRO. This time Pizarro has overstepped his bounds.

DE SOTO. I agree wholeheartedly. After returning from Spain I was furious to learn of the Inca's execution.

ALMAGRO. I also am furious with the limpet.

DE SOTO. What's a limpet?

ALMAGRO. I don't know. It sounds good, doesn't it? As I was saying, I was so mad at Pizarro. He cheated me. I should have received an equal reward. I fought more than he. I plundered more than he. But he took it all away from me. He's nothing but a power hungry limpet.

DE SOTO. And now look at him. The poor swindler who can't even read is going around all hoity-toity in that high falootin way giving orders left and right. Fair isn't in his dictionary!

ALMAGRO. We need to take him down a peg or two.

DE SOTO. Or three?

ALMAGRO. Might as well take him down all the way.

(*They both take a sip of their root beers and slam their cups down as if in agreement.* **DE SOTO** *exits one direction and* **PIZARRO** *walks in from the other direction and sees an angry* **ALMAGRO**.)

PIZARRO. Why, hello Diego. Not still stewing over the proclamation are you?

ALMAGRO. Yes, I am stewing! I want my share of the gold! I want my share of power! I speak what your men are afraid to!

PIZARRO. Why are they afraid?

ALMAGRO. Because monster that you are, you would unfeelingly execute anyone who dared to complain about your traitorous ways.

PIZARRO. Precisely. Ruiz!

*(**RUIZ** enters.)*

RUIZ. What is it, sir?

PIZARRO. Arrest my old friend here and tell the executioner to prepare for another one.

ALMAGRO. What? You little…!

RUIZ. Another killing? And now your closest friend? When will you stop? No, sir. I will not do this evil thing! You can tell me to serve you wine, draw your bath, blow your nose, dance the macarena, whatever, but I will have no part in this wickedness. I defy you.

*(**RUIZ** storms off.)*

PIZARRO. Manco!

*(**MANCO** enters.)*

Arrest this man and execute him! The sooner the better.

MANCO. Yes, master. *(to the audience)* One less Spaniard to oppose our freedom.

*(**MANCO** and **ALMAGRO** exit.)*

PIZARRO. Well, well. I am sole ruler of this realm now! Nothing stands in my way! My only superior is thousands of miles away and this country leaps to do my bidding! At last real power and wealth are MINE, MINE, MINE!

*(**PIZARRO** exits.)*

Scene 10:
The Bar

(FRANCISCO ALMAGRO, ALMAGRO's son, is leading a revolt. DE SOTO and RUIZ are there too. MANCO pours drinks and listens in.)

RUIZ. I witnessed Diego de Almagro asking for his equal partnership and Pizarro tells me to execute his best friend! I flat out refused and ran away, fearing my own life.

F. ALMAGRO. I must avenge my father's death! Pizarro is a disgrace to our country. He may have conquered lands for the King but he is ruthless to his own countrymen! I move we attack!

ALL. *(as they draw swords)* Aye!!

MANCO. *(surprising the rest of them)* Let me in on this. I too am weary of Pizarro's rule. Let me distract him, and my countrymen will assist.

F. ALMAGRO. It's settled. Go, men!

ALL. Yea!!

(All run offstage, swords drawn.)

Scene 11:
Pizarro's Room Near a Window

(**PIZARRO** *is wearing robes, gold around him, staring out his window at "his" city.* **MANCO** *enters.*)

PIZARRO. Ah, Manco. Take a look at my new city – Lima.

MANCO. Gorgeous, my lord.

(**SPANIARDS** *enter.*)

He's all yours boys.

PIZARRO. De Soto? Ruiz? Traitors!

DE SOTO. No more than you are! You killed your friend. Your selfish lust will wreck the Spanish chance of a hold in Peru!

F. ALMAGRO. My name is Francisco Almagro. You killed my father! Prepare to die.

(*A sword fight ensues,* **PIZARRO** *disarms* **DE SOTO**. **F. ALMAGRO** *jumps in and stabs* **PIZARRO**. **MARIA** *enters.*)

MARIA. UNCLE!! Oh Uncle. Why could you not see? Your greed has ruined you.

PIZARRO. (*dying*) Maria, my niece. My deeds have killed me. I offer no excuse. I guess there is no gold where I am headed now…Adios.

(**MARIA** *weeps.*)

F. ALMAGRO. He is gone.

(*There is silence.*)

DE SOTO. I think the world is better off now. Let us all take this lesson of greed to heart.

(*They all bow heads and cross themselves.*)